Princess for a Week

Betty Ren Wright

illustrated by
Jacqueline Rogers

Holiday House / New York

/

3   5   7   9   10   8   6   4   2

Library of Congress Cataloging-in-Publication Data

Wright, Betty Ren.
  Princess for a week / by Betty Ren Wright ; illustrated by Jacqueline Rogers.— 1st ed.
    p. cm.
  Summary: When a confident girl named Princess arrives to spend a week at Roddy's
house, she encourages him to help her investigate the suspicious activities happening at a
supposedly haunted house.
  ISBN-10: 0-8234-1945-2
  ISBN-13: 978-0-8234-1945-6
  [1. Haunted houses—Fiction.   2. Ghosts—Fiction.   3. Mystery and detective stories.]
I. Rogers, Jacqueline, ill.   II. Title.

PZ7.W933Pri   2006
[Fic]—dc22
                    2005050288

For Shirley, Jane, Betty Ruth,
Pat, Bunny, Joyce, Louise, and
Janet, who have made me forever
grateful to have been
a Downer girl

Contents

1. Day One

"It's way too big, Roddy," Jacob said. "It won't fit."

Roddy Hall stared at the doghouse. The battered old wreck, tilted against the side of the wagon, looked as if it might fall apart at any moment. Still, he had to have it. Once he got it home, he'd figure out how to fix it.

"All you have to do is hold the wagon steady for a sec," he said. "I'll slide the house up over the edge, and then we can sort of balance it."

Jacob rolled his eyes but did as he was told. Roddy shoved, grunted, and shoved again. Gradually the house moved upward. Then it crashed down across the wagon, sticking out on either side.

"Beautiful!" Roddy puffed, picking up a board that had fallen off the roof. "You hold it in place, and I'll pull the wagon."

They walked slowly up the gravel road from the

1

riverbank where someone had dumped the dog-house. Roddy had noticed it two months ago, right after he and his mom moved to Hilltop Drive. For a few days he had wandered around alone, just look-ing at the many empty, run-down houses. His mom always said Hilltop was the right place to be because the rent was so low. She liked it, too, because the town was just eight miles from Gregg Army Base. His dad had left for Afghanistan from Gregg, and it was the place he would return to someday.

"Make the best of it," his mom had said. "You never know what's waiting for you out there, little man."

Now he knew that the doghouse had been wait-ing, like a miracle, when he needed one. Maybe this would be a whole week of miracles. The doghouse today, and tomorrow or the day after a letter or an e-mail from his dad to say he would be home soon. Roddy pulled harder, just thinking about it.

"You don't even know for sure you're getting a dog," Jacob grumbled. "We might be doing all this work for nothing."

"I do know for sure." Roddy corrected him. "I was there when my mom's friend Linda called this morning. She shows dogs for rich people, and she's taking one to a show in Philadelphia today. Her neighbor's supposed to come in and look after things when Linda's away, but the neighbor has the flu. So Linda needs someone to take care of her own dog, Princess, for a week. My mom said okay. And," Roddy finished triumphantly, "the minute I heard that I remembered this doghouse."

"Still a lot of work for one week," Jacob mumbled.

Roddy didn't argue. He'd wanted a dog for as long as he could remember. Now he had a week to prove to his mom that he was old enough to take care of one himself.

"You taking that thing to the dump?"

Both boys jumped. Neither one had noticed the girl coming toward them.

"Want some help?" she asked coolly. "I don't mind."

"No, thanks," Roddy said.

"Sure," Jacob said.

"I'll push," the girl announced, as if she hadn't heard Roddy at all. She was skinny and brown, with a long, almost white braid and startling blue eyes. She wore a baggy T-shirt with SAVE THE PLANET EARTH printed on it.

They started up the hill. Roddy pulled, the girl pushed, and Jacob kept both hands on the doghouse to keep it from slipping.

"How far to the dump?" the girl demanded.

Roddy pretended not to hear.

"We're going to Roddy's house," Jacob ex-

plained. "He's getting a dog, and it's going to need a house."

The girl snorted. "That poor dog will drown in the first rainstorm," she said. "Look at the roof."

"The roof will be fine," Roddy snapped. "I've got plans."

The wagon began to move faster. Soon Roddy almost had to run to keep ahead of it. When he looked back he saw that Jacob was running, too. The girl was out of sight behind the wagon, but when she spoke again she wasn't panting at all.

"I'd never make a dog sleep in a doghouse," she said. "I'd have it in my bedroom. Right on my bed."

What a pain she was! "Stop pushing," Roddy growled. "This is where I live."

The girl's head popped up from behind the doghouse. "You're kidding!" she exclaimed. "You're Roddy Hall? I didn't know you were getting a dog. That's great!"

"The dog isn't here yet," Roddy told her. "She's coming today."

"Princess," Jacob added. "That's her name."

The girl's blue eyes narrowed. She looked at Jacob, then at Roddy. Then she looked down at the doghouse.

"You are *so* not bright," she said. "I'm Princess. Princess Thornberry. My stepmother Linda dropped me off an hour ago. And if you think I'm going to sleep in a broken-down doghouse, you're crazy. Your mom said I get the bedroom with all the dinosaur posters."

Roddy blinked. "Now just wait," he sputtered. "You're not—you can't—you're not a dog."

"Smart kid," the girl said. "You should be a detective."

Roddy was stunned. Whoever heard of a girl called Princess? "I don't believe you," he said faintly.

"I do." Jacob sighed. "I just knew we were doing all this work for nothing." He poked Roddy with his elbow. "That's your bedroom she's talking about," he said. "The bedroom with all the dinosaur posters. Maybe you're the one who gets to sleep in the doghouse tonight."

2. Night One

"It's not my fault you misunderstood," Roddy's mother said in a low voice. She smoothed a blanket over the cot in the basement. "You should have asked me, little man. Her real name is Jane, but her father started calling her Princess when she was a baby, and the name stuck."

Roddy sat down on the cot with a *thump*. "Well, she's not a princess to me," he muttered. "Why does she have to sleep in my room?"

"Because the family-room couch is lumpy," his mom said calmly. "As you very well know. And I wouldn't ask our guest—a sweet little girl—to sleep in the basement." She reached across the cot and tousled his hair. "You have the camp lantern and your radio—you'll be fine. It's only for a week, Roddy. Have a good night now."

At the top of the stairs she turned off the light,

and Roddy switched on the camp lantern. A pool of light sprang up around the cot, but the rest of the basement was full of hulking shadows. The furnace. The water heater. Piles of still-packed boxes. Across the room a faint light streamed in through the small window, making the washer and dryer gleam spookily.

Roddy lay down and pulled the sheet and blanket up to his chin. He wondered if his dad slept on a cot like this one. When his father went to Afghanistan, at first he had been stationed in an abandoned hotel. He'd drawn a funny picture of the hotel in one of his letters. Then he had e-mailed to say he was being moved. Soon after that the messages had stopped.

"I bet he's in a palace now," Roddy's mom had joked. "He hasn't written because he doesn't want to make us jealous." But when she said that her smile was kind of lopsided, and she kept reading the old letters over and over again, as if she were looking for something that wasn't there.

Roddy moved the lantern closer and switched it off. The basement was very dark. Princess! he thought disgustedly. Old Princess was probably propped up in his bed watching his television. He squirmed, remembering how eager she'd been to tell his mom about the doghouse.

"He thought I was a dog!" she'd snickered, and his mom had chuckled, too—just a little, but still. . . .

8

He pulled the blanket higher and tried to forget how much he'd wanted that dog. Even for a week.

His dad wouldn't have laughed.

One minute he was sort of floating down Hilltop Drive, his feet not quite touching the road, and there was a beautiful golden retriever loping along beside him. The next minute he was sitting up straight on the cot, too scared to breathe. An odd sound had awakened him—a muffled thud, followed by a scuffling noise. He reached for the lantern, but before he could turn it on, someone ran by outside the moonlit window.

A robber! he thought. A guy who knew his dad had shipped out and thought it would be easy to break in.

He felt around in the dark for his shoes and tip-toed up the stairs. The door at the top opened into the little back hall. Roddy stood very still, his heart thumping like a drum inside his chest. Then he slid his fingers across the opposite wall, until he found his baseball bat propped in the corner. He hoisted it to his shoulder and unlocked the door.

The world outside wasn't as dark as the basement had been. Roddy tiptoed to the front of the house and peeked around the corner. No one on the front porch. No one moving at all. He began to feel a little braver.

I would have smacked him if I'd caught him,

he'd tell Jacob tomorrow. Even if he'd been a great big guy, I would have knocked him out. If that happened there might be a picture in the paper of this kid protecting his house and his mother. They could send the picture to Afghanistan . . . his dad would be proud.

Something hit him on the head and rolled out onto the street. Roddy's hands turned clammy. He squinted and saw that it was an apple—one of the small green ones that dotted the tree in front of his house.

"You are just weird," said a voice from the tree. "Who else plays baseball in the middle of the night?"

The girl—Princess—was high in the tree, straddling a branch, her legs swinging. Like she couldn't fall if she tried, Roddy thought. He hated high places himself.

"You're supposed to be in bed," he said in a growly whisper. "My mom would be really mad if she knew you sneaked out."

"That's why I was very quiet," Princess said. "So I wouldn't disturb her."

"Well, I heard you," Roddy said. "I thought someone was trying to break into our house."

"And you were going to hit him with the bat?" She sounded as if he'd said something funny, but

she didn't actually laugh. "Come on up here," she said. "You can see everything."

"What's there to see?" Roddy demanded. "It's the middle of the night!" He felt really stupid, standing there in his pj's, holding a baseball bat and talking to a tree. "You'd better get back in the house before you break your neck."

"No way," Princess said.

Roddy scowled. He couldn't make her come down, and he was pretty sure his mom wouldn't want him to leave her outside. He was still trying to decide what to do, when Princess said, "Hey!" and stopped swinging her legs. "There's a car coming down the hill. With no headlights! How strange is that?"

Pretty strange, Roddy admitted to himself. He moved closer to the tree trunk and peered around it at the hulking, almost silent car. It moved slowly. When it turned in at the driveway two houses farther up the hill on the other side of the street, his heart gave a nasty little lurch. He knew all about that house, because Jacob had told him. It was haunted.

"With no lights," Princess repeated. "We have to sneak up there and see what's going on."

"Not a chance," Roddy said, trying to keep his voice steady. "Who cares what they're doing?"

He had hardly gotten the words out when

Princess came shinnying down the tree like a monkey.

"That really could be a burglar," she whispered. "Why else would they be so quiet and not have any lights?" She grabbed Roddy's arm and pulled. "Don't be scared, Roddy. I thought that was why you came outside with a baseball bat—to catch a burglar."

Roddy gritted his teeth. He wished he'd fallen asleep the minute his mom turned out the light. He wished he'd never come outside. He wished—more than anything—that Princess had turned out to be a dog.

3. Day Two

"So then what happened?" Jacob demanded. "Hurry up, man!"

They were sitting on the ground behind the garage, out of sight of the house and any nosy girl visitor who might be wandering around.

"Nothing happened," Roddy told him. "My mom switched on the light in the kitchen—she gets up to get a glass of milk if she can't sleep—and I said that meant she might be wandering around for hours. I said she'd probably check on Princess, and when she saw that empty bed . . ." He grinned, remembering how quickly Princess had given up the idea of investigating the car. "But she's going to want to go poking around that house later," he went on. "I could tell. And she's going to want us to go with her."

"Us?" Jacob repeated. "What do you mean, us? I told you that house is haunted. I'm not going anywhere near it."

Roddy scooped up a handful of pebbles and tossed them across the alley. He thought about the car moving without headlights down the hill.

"How do you know it's haunted?" he asked, although he already knew the answer.

"My great-uncle Ringwald told me," Jacob said. "And he knows about stuff like that. He's seen lots of ghosts. He's talked to 'em. He really knows."

Roddy leaned back against the garage and groaned. He didn't want to hear this.

"Ask him yourself, if you don't believe me," Jacob said, sounding annoyed. "Let's go ask him right now." He stood up, and Roddy got up, too, because he didn't know what else to do. He didn't want Jacob to be mad at him.

They walked slowly up the alley to Jacob's house at the top of the hill. Jacob opened the rickety gate and led the way around the garage into the narrow backyard. It was a nice yard. Pink and red holly-hocks teetered along one fence, leaning against one another for support. In front of them, vegetables grew in neat rows. Roddy hadn't been in Jacob's backyard often—they usually played at the foot of the hill along the stream—but he liked it there. This was the kind of yard he wanted if he and his folks ever settled down to stay in one place.

A picnic table stood close to the house, and on the table was what looked like a huge heap of old clothes.

"There he is," Jacob said in a low voice. "He always takes a nap out here after breakfast. My mom says it gives her time to straighten up his room."

"We'd better not bother him," Roddy said quickly. "I'll ask about the house some other time."

The pile of clothes shifted on the table, and Uncle Ring's huge bearded face rose to look at them. He didn't speak, just watched as they crossed the yard. Then he swung his feet over the side of the table and nodded.

"What are you fellas up to today?" he rumbled. "And who's your friend?"

"You know Roddy, Uncle Ring," Jacob said. "The new kid down the block. He's been here before."

"'Course I know him," Uncle Ring said gruffly. "I know everybody around here. I didn't mean him. Who's that long drink of water back by the gate?"

Both boys whirled around. No one was there.

"There's nobody—" Roddy said, but Jacob interrupted.

"What's he look like, Uncle Ring?"

Uncle Ring didn't seem surprised by the question. He tilted his head and narrowed his eyes. "Fine lookin' fella," he said finally. "Army uniform, looks like." He paused. "He's going now. Guess he just stopped by to say hello. Can you think who he was?"

17

Roddy could hardly breathe. "No!" he gasped. "I don't know any ghosts."

Uncle Ring looked startled. "Well now, I never said he was a ghost, did I? That wasn't a ghost at all. Sometimes people travel in their thoughts, and if you have my kind of eyes you can see 'em. Happens all the time."

"Roddy's dad is in the army," Jacob said, looking uneasy. "He's overseas."

"Well, there you are." Uncle Ring leaned back on the table, supporting his huge bulk on one elbow. "That proves what I said. Your dad's thinkin' about home all the time, and right now he was just checkin' up to make sure you're okay." He yawned. "Guess I'll sleep a little longer, if you don't want anything special."

"Roddy wants to ask you something," Jacob said hurriedly. "About that house across the street. It's haunted, isn't it? You said it was."

"You bet your lucky penny it's haunted," Uncle Ring said sleepily. He lay back and closed his eyes. "There's been a ghost in that old place for forty years."

"But somebody lives there," Roddy said. "I saw his car last night."

"People move in and stay a little while and move right out again," Uncle Ring said. "Don't blame 'em a bit. There's ghosts and then there's ghosts—good ones and bad ones. That place has the worst kind—mean as poison. . . ." The sentence trailed off, ending in a snore so loud that the boys jumped.

"Let's get out of here," Roddy said. He headed back to the gate and looked both ways before stepping out into the alley.

"So what do you think?" Jacob asked when he'd caught up. "Uncle Ring sure knows about ghosts and haunted houses, right?"

"I guess," Roddy said. But he no longer cared about the house across the street. All he could think about was the figure Uncle Ring had seen at the gate. Could it have been his dad? Was it possible that a person might travel halfway around the world in his thoughts? Or was the figure something else, and Uncle Ring was just trying to be kind?

Roddy felt sick. Uncle Ring was the big ghost expert. He could see ghosts, and maybe that's what he'd just seen. Maybe that was why there hadn't been any messages from Afghanistan for a while.

4. Night Two

"You kids have fun," Roddy's mom said. "I'll take care of the dishes."

Roddy headed toward the television set and his favorite video game, but, for once, Princess didn't follow him. "Linda said I should help you, Mrs. Hall," she said. "I'm a very good dishwasher."

"So what else is new?" Roddy grumbled to himself. Does she have to be the best at *everything*?

He and Jacob had spent the afternoon finding out just how good Princess was. No matter how hard they tried to get away from her, she always found them. She could run faster than they could. She could scramble over a fence without half trying. She could catch a softball and throw it back so fast you couldn't see it coming. When she asked who wanted to wrestle, Jacob went home.

Thunder rumbled through the living-room screen door. The curtains rose and fell in the breeze.

Roddy took out the video game, then put it back. There was something else he wanted to do, now, without Princess trailing after him.

All afternoon the conversation with Uncle Ring had buzzed like a bee in the back of his head. Talking to Jacob had helped a little. Being mad at Princess had helped, too. But tonight, as he sat across from his mom at the supper table, he'd felt just awful. Would she be smiling if she knew about the tall man in the army uniform? He thought if he could just catch a glimpse of the man himself, he'd know whether it really was his father and whether it was a ghost.

He opened the screen door and stepped out onto the porch. Down the hill a woman called her dog. Up the hill and across the street a tall willow dipped and danced in the wind. The willow marked the front yard of the haunted house, hiding the dark bulk behind it.

Quickly, before he could lose his nerve, Roddy walked around the side of his house and across the backyard. The alley looked strange and a little frightening in the half dark, but he was ready for that. If there was a chance—even a little one—he wanted to see the tall man for himself.

Lightning lit up the sky, and the thunder that followed was very loud. In the flash of light, Roddy thought he saw something move up the alley near

Jacob's backyard. He leaned against the garage, hardly breathing. When the lightning cracked again, he was ready, staring at the spot.

A garage door swung in the wind. That was all.

"What are you *doing* out here?" said a voice behind him, so close that he jumped. Princess looked at him curiously.

"None of your business," Roddy snapped. "I'm just looking around."

"At what?" Princess stepped backward, not waiting for an answer. "Your mother thinks you're down in the basement, but I saw you sneak across the yard."

"I wasn't sneaking," Roddy said. He looked once more up the alley and then headed back to the house. Raindrops peppered his face.

"If it rains all night, I'm going to be so mad!" Princess exclaimed. "We'll get soaked when we check out that house."

Roddy walked faster. "We're not checking out that house," he mumbled. "Just forget it."

"Not a chance," Princess said. "I'm going to find out what's going on over there, and then I'm going to call the police. And the newspaper," she added grandly. "They can take my picture if they want to."

"They won't want to," Roddy said, trying not to

remember he'd had the same idea the night before. Catching a criminal had seemed almost possible then, but that was before he had talked to Uncle Ring. There was a mean ghost in that house—the worst kind. Uncle Ring knew things.

Later, when Roddy picked up the camp lantern and went downstairs to bed, his mom followed him. Rain was coming down hard, rattling closed-up windows and drumming on the glass. His mom fluffed up his pillow and gave him a hug when he lay down on the cot.

"It's good of you to let Princess hang out with you," she said softly. "I feel so sorry for her."

"Sorry for her!" Roddy was amazed. "You don't have to feel sorry for *her*. She can do anything. Ask her, she'll tell you."

"I'm guessing she's a pretty lonely little girl," his mom said. "She adores her father, but he's in Europe on business for months at a time. She's in boarding school all year, except for holidays. I know Linda is a good person, but she's more comfortable with dogs than with kids. It's really nice for Princess to be part of our family for a few days. She's never had a brother or a sister to play with."

The words bounced around in Roddy's head after his mom had gone back upstairs and turned out the light. She was all wrong about Princess.

That kid didn't need anyone to feel sorry for her. And she didn't want a brother to play with, she just wanted someone to boss around.

He snuggled deeper under the covers and closed his eyes. At once his thoughts went back to the figure Uncle Ring had seen in the alley—the "long drink of water" in the army uniform. If what Uncle Ring said was true, then his dad could be here in the basement right now, making sure everything was all right. "Not my father's ghost"—he told himself hurriedly—"not *that*." Uncle Ring knew the difference.

Thunder shook the house, followed by a sharp *tap-tap* close by. Roddy's eyes flew open. Another flash of lightning, and he saw Princess crouched at the window.

He groaned. No one, not even Princess, could be dumb enough to go prowling around in this storm. He closed his eyes again, scrunching them tight.

Tap-tap. Okay, so she really was that dumb. He turned his back to the window and waited.

She tapped twice more, and then, when at last he sneaked a look at the window, it was empty. Good, he thought. She'd given up and gone back to bed. But even as he thought it, he knew it wasn't true. That girl was as stubborn as a donkey. And since he knew she was out there, and he knew where she was going, it would be all his fault if she got into trouble.

She was waiting near the front of the house, pressed against the wet siding.

"Well, finally!" she said, not even sounding surprised that he'd come. "I have a flashlight, so we can look in the windows."

Roddy squinted into the dark. "Hey, that's *my* flashlight!" he exclaimed. "Who said you could poke around in my stuff?"

Princess started across the street, ignoring the rain. "I didn't poke around in your stuff, goofy. Your mother emptied out a dresser drawer so I could have room for my things."

Roddy walked faster to keep up with the girl's long strides. His sneakers squished through the little rivers racing down Hilltop Drive.

"Listen," he said. "You can't sneak around that house. You could be arrested or shot or—something. It might be dangerous."

"I know," she agreed, surprising him. "That's why we have to do it. We have to catch the bad guys."

Roddy grabbed her shirt and pulled her to a stop. "That's not what I mean," he said. "It could be a whole lot worse than bad guys."

"Bad guys with guns," Princess said. "What's worse than that?"

Roddy gulped. "I'll tell you what's worse," he said desperately. "That house is haunted! It's the truth. I know for sure!"

Princess glanced at the dark house. It looked bigger than it did in the daytime. Scarier, too, Roddy thought, but then, everything looked scary in a storm.

"You are such a wimp," she said. "I can't even believe you said such a wimpy thing."

Just then, headlights appeared at the top of the hill. The car drifted slowly toward them. As it neared, a spotlight came on and swept back and forth across the street.

Roddy remembered a deer he had seen one night when he was with his dad in their car. The deer had just stood there in the light, not daring to move. He knew how that deer had felt.

"Now you've done it," Princess growled as the car rolled to a stop. "Hanging around out here talking, for Pete's sake! You and your stupid ghosts!"

But her voice quivered just a little, Roddy noticed, and she moved closer to him as the car door opened and a policeman stepped out into the rain.

5. Day Three

In the wet, roaring darkness, the policeman looked eight feet tall. He stared down at Roddy and Princess as if they were creatures from outer space.

"Now what's all this?" he demanded. "Do your folks know you're out here? It's after midnight and the sky is falling, in case you haven't noticed."

Roddy wished he could melt and float away down the hill. They were in big trouble now, with no way out.

"It's my cat," Princess said, and all of a sudden her voice was whimpery and sweet. "My poor kitty. He's out here somewhere, all by himself. We have to find him."

"Your cat?" the policeman repeated. A tiny waterfall poured from the brim of his hat. "You're out in this storm looking for your cat! Where do you kids live, anyway?"

"Right there." Roddy pointed. "I mean, I live there—she's just visiting."

"With my little kitty," Princess said sadly. "Only he got away. And he's my dearest, dearest friend." She sounded ready to cry.

"Well, you aren't going to find him tonight," the policeman said. "Cats are smart—he's hiding in a nice dry place, and he's going to stay there until it stops raining. So that's what you two better do, right now! Go home! I'll come with you."

"No!" Roddy squawked. "You can't!"

"You can't!" Princess repeated in her teary voice.

"Is that so!" The policeman bent down, and a regular Niagara Falls poured off the visor. "Your folks ought to know what you've been up to."

Princess talked very fast. "You can't because you'll scare his mother to death. His dad is overseas fighting and she's awful worried all the time. That's why we didn't tell about my cat, see? We didn't want to make her feel worse."

The policeman rolled his eyes. Then he grabbed their shoulders and turned them around. "Okay, that's enough," he said. "Just go! And don't come back outside or I'll take you both down to the station. Got that?"

Roddy ran. "Got it," he heard Princess say. And then she added unbelievably, "If you see a black and white kitty, he's mine. His name is Roddy and he's scared of *everything*."

* * *

Jacob was waiting behind the garage when Roddy slipped out the next morning. He gave a sigh of relief when he saw that Roddy was alone.

"She's making chocolate chip cookies with my mom," Roddy said sourly. "She wants to learn how so she can make them for her father when he comes home from his big important business trip next weekend."

They started up the hill, and Roddy told Jacob what had happened the night before. "So besides everything else, she's a liar," he finished up. "The biggest liar I've ever met! And my mom thinks she's perfect. I can tell."

"*She* thinks she's perfect, too," Jacob said. "That makes two of them."

Roddy sighed. Between the storm and the close call with the policeman, he'd hardly slept the rest of the night. He wished he could believe that Princess would give up investigating the haunted house now, but he knew she wouldn't. She'd as good as said so at breakfast that morning.

"I tried to make chocolate chip cookies at home," she'd told Roddy's mom. "But they burned. Linda said there might be something wrong with our oven."

"Well, you can try it again today," Roddy's mom said, giving her a little hug. "You mustn't give up."

"Oh, I won't," Princess said, and then she'd

30

turned to look straight at Roddy. "*I* never, ever give up."

"She wasn't talking about cookies when she said that," Roddy told Jacob. "She's just weird!"

"You betcha," Jacob said. "Plain crazy! And if you keep tagging after her at night, you're crazy, too."

They found Uncle Ring on Jacob's front porch swing. His eyes were closed, but they flew open when the boys came up the steps.

"Well, now," he said cheerfully, "too bad you fellas didn't come by a few minutes ago. You missed someone worth seeing."

Roddy felt that same little jump in his heart. "Was it the soldier?"

"It was Mrs. Mortimer," Uncle Ring said. "Fresh as a daisy, like she never had a sick day in her life. She waved to me."

"Mrs. Mortimer used to live next door to us," Jacob whispered. "She died last summer."

"What a treat to see her again!" Uncle Ring said. "She was a good old soul."

Roddy sat down hard on the top step. He felt a little dizzy. "About that house across the street," he said shakily. "You said there's a mean ghost in there. Why is he mean, do you think?"

"Because he wants to keep people away, I expect," Uncle Ring said. "Same as he did when he

was alive. They say he has a ton of money hidden away in there."

"But you told us other people have lived there since the mean guy died," Roddy said. "The money's probably gone by now."

"Never heard of anyone finding a treasure." Uncle Ring yawned. "No, it's still in there someplace, and so is he—forty years or more. I can feel waves of meanness pourin' out of that place this very minute. Pure meanness!"

The branches of the willow in front of the haunted house swayed ever so slightly. Roddy stared down at the sidewalk. An ant was dragging a crumb that was bigger than it was.

"Well, now," Uncle Ring said suddenly. He leaned forward on the swing. "Look there, will you. If she ain't a sight for sore eyes!"

Roddy froze. He kept his eyes on the ant. "Is it Mrs. Mortimer?" he asked Jacob under his breath.

"Worse," Jacob whispered back. "It's her—Princess."

The ant crawled into the grass and vanished.

Reluctantly, Roddy looked up and saw Princess across the street and down a ways. Her long braid gleamed in the sunlight as she ambled back and forth, studying the haunted house.

"Never saw that one around here before," Uncle Ring said. "Jacob, she looks a lot like your mama did when she was a little girl. That shiny hair and all. What's she eatin', I wonder?"

"It's an absolutely perfect chocolate chip cookie," Roddy said bitterly. "Take my word for it."

"She must have just moved in down the block," Uncle Ring said. "I bet she's lonesome, poor kid. You fellas will have to look after her. Show her around. You hear, Jacob?"

"Yeah." Jacob slid off the steps, and Roddy followed. They waved good-bye to Uncle Ring and zoomed around the side of the house, bumping into each other as they ran.

"It doesn't make any difference," Jacob said as soon as they were safely in the alley. "Uncle Ring saying that, I mean. She's staying at *your* house. She's *your* problem."

Roddy grinned. He felt better than he had since Princess arrived. "Sure it makes a difference," he said. "He's your uncle Ring, and he knows stuff. If she gets in trouble now, it'll be your fault as much as mine. He said look after her, so you have to do it."

"Do not," Jacob said weakly.

"Do, too." Roddy took a deep breath. Maybe it wouldn't be quite so scary tonight, he thought, with Jacob along.

6. Night Three

"We're going to hide under those bushes along the driveway," Princess whispered. "There's a whole row of them. I checked it out this afternoon. If the robber comes back tonight, we'll get a good look at him."

Boss, boss, boss, Roddy thought. "What if he goes up the alley and parks in the garage?"

"We'll still see him when he comes to the house. But he can't park in there. I looked through the garage window this afternoon. The place is full of junk—an old tractor, firewood, stuff like that. He has to park in the little driveway that goes to the side door."

She darted across the dark street, and Roddy and Jacob followed more slowly.

"This is so dumb," Jacob muttered, just loud enough to be heard. "My uncle said we should stay away from this place."

Princess glared over her shoulder. "I hope you didn't tell your uncle anything," she said sharply. "We're on a secret investigation, Jacob. You're lucky I'm letting you come along."

"Yeah," Jacob said. "Lucky me."

"Just do what she says," Roddy whispered. "It's easier."

He had been almost glad when Princess rapped on the basement window tonight. Going on a secret investigation was better than lying awake, thinking about Mrs. Mortimer and the tall man in the army uniform. Mrs. Mortimer was dead. The tall man was not. Uncle Ring said so, but how could he be so sure?

Jacob had been waiting for them in the shadows next to his house. "Just do everything I say," Princess had said, and ignored Jacob's groan.

"Okay," she said, "now here's where we go undercover." She dropped to her knees and vanished under a lilac bush close to the drive. "Follow me," her voice came out of the dark. "Don't make any noise."

Roddy felt a little thrill of excitement. Leaves, still damp from the rain of the night before, tickled the back of his neck as he crawled. He started to sneeze but didn't. Undercover, he thought. That sounded important.

"Why can't we just walk?" Jacob complained. "There's nobody here now."

"Shhh." Princess kept crawling, then stopped so suddenly that Roddy's nose bumped her shoe. He rocked back and touched a finger to his upper lip, feeling for blood. Injured in the line of duty, he thought, but there wasn't any.

"Go a little bit farther," Jacob whispered. "I'm sitting in a puddle."

Princess didn't move. "This is where the car will stop, so we have to stay right here. Besides, if you get too comfortable, you might fall asleep."

"Fall asleep?" Jacob gasped. "Fall asleep! Don't make jokes."

Roddy poked his head out from under a branch that was blocking his view. The haunted house loomed forbiddingly on the other side of the gravel drive. Someone could be staring out at him right now, he thought, and he wouldn't know it. Someone mean, who had been staring out those dark windows for forty years, watching, waiting. . . .

"Hey!" He scuttled back under the bush, bumping into Jacob this time. "I saw something—a light!" he gasped. "Just for a sec!"

"I told you," Jacob moaned. "Uncle Ring said—"

"You did not see a light," Princess said, forgetting to whisper. "You couldn't. There's no one in there. Not yet."

"It wasn't a *big* light," Roddy said, "but I saw it.

That window nearest the front of the house. Sort of a glimmer."

"A *glimmer*," Jacob repeated. "A glimmer? You know what glimmers? A ghost glimmers, that's what! I'm out of here!" He scrambled out from under the bushes and raced down the drive to the street.

"Now you did it," Princess said crossly. "You and your glimmer! If anyone sees Jacob, we're never going to get a chance to solve the mystery."

Roddy's heart pounded. He didn't blame Jacob for running—he wanted to run, too. But had he really seen a glimmer? He thought so. He was almost certain.

"Well, how long are we going to wait, anyway?" he asked miserably. "There must be about a million mosquitoes under here."

"When we saw the car the other night, it was about ten-thirty," Princess said, like she'd been just waiting for him to ask. "I know because I looked at my watch before I came outside. The thief probably works on some kind of schedule. He breaks into a place and then he comes here to hide his loot. That's his MO. I figure if he's coming, he'll be here before midnight."

Roddy was impressed. She had it all worked out. "What's an 'emmo'?"

"That's the way a robber works, dopey. His

method of operating. Every criminal has an MO. Don't you watch television?"

Roddy peeked out again at the front window. That would be the living room, he thought. Why would a ghost go glimmering around a living room? Ghosts hang out in attics and basements, don't they? He leaned back and slapped a mosquito, or something bigger, off his cheek.

A long time later, after he'd been dinner for a hundred *more* mosquitoes, Princess finally sighed and said, "Well, okay. He's not coming tonight." She gave Roddy a little push and started crawling back toward the street.

"If he's not coming, why do we have to—" Roddy began and then gave up. At least they were going home. She'd have her reasons why they had to crawl—some stupid *emmo* reason that would make him feel dumber than ever.

Later, back in the basement, with nothing to do but think and scratch, he heard footsteps overhead. His mother was out in the kitchen opening and closing the refrigerator, her slippers flip-flopping across the linoleum. Then she was in the living room, right over his head. The front door opened and closed very softly.

Roddy hated to think of her out on the porch in the dark, worrying about his dad. That's what she was doing, he knew. Every day without a letter made it worse. *Tomorrow I'll tell her he's okay,* he thought. *I'll tell her Uncle Ring saw him.* At the same time he knew he wouldn't say anything at all. He wasn't sure of the truth himself.

To his surprise, when he went upstairs the next morning, his mom looked pretty cheerful.

"I sat outside for the longest time last night," she said softly. "It was nice. There's something kind of magical about a summer night, did you know that? Your dad seemed so close, Roddy." She smiled at him, and then at Princess. "I actually felt as if he might come walking down the hill any minute, looking just the way he did the last time we saw him."

Roddy stared at her. *The tall man in an army uniform.* He didn't know what to say.

Neither did Princess, for once. Roddy knew what *she* was thinking. "What—what time were you out there?" she finally asked in a choked voice. "Did you see—were there any kids around?"

"Of course not, hon—it was very late." His mom looked puzzled. "What would kids be doing outside at that hour?"

"Right," Princess said. She went back to buttering her toast, making sure that the raspberry jam was spread evenly over every bit of it. Roddy reached for his glass of orange juice.

"I did see one odd thing, though," his mom went on thoughtfully. "A car turned into that old house across the street—the one with the willow tree in front. I didn't think anyone lived there. He must have been having a problem of some kind—the head- lights weren't on."

Roddy's glass of orange juice slipped through his fingers. He reached out to grab it just as Prin- cess's toast landed on the table, jam side down.

7. Day Four

"We're having a picnic—hot dogs and chips and stuff," Jacob said. "Just Uncle Ring and me. Do you want to come? My folks are working all day at our church fair." He looked uncertainly from Roddy to Princess. Roddy could tell he was sorry he'd run off and left them the night before.

When they didn't answer, Roddy's mom spoke up.

"Well, I think that's very nice of you, Jacob," she said. "Are you sure your mother expects you to invite friends?"

Jacob nodded. "She said as long as I was going to baby sit Uncle Ring all day I might as well have company."

"Baby sit?" Princess looked interested for the first time. "What's wrong with your uncle?"

"He's my *great*-uncle," Jacob said. "And there's nothing wrong with him. I'm just supposed to see that he—that he doesn't get lonesome. Or excited. He gets sick when he's too excited." He turned to Roddy. "We have a whole box of chocolate-nut ice-cream bars."

Roddy could feel his mom's look as she waited for him to speak. "Well, okay," he said, pretending the chocolate-nut ice-cream bars had made up his mind. Actually, he didn't want to stay mad at Jacob. In another couple of days Princess would be gone, like a bad cold, and then they could start having fun again.

As the three of them started up the alley, Roddy told Jacob that the car without headlights had come back.

"And that proves what I told you," Princess said. "Whoever it is, he's doing something bad he doesn't want people around here to know about. Only we're too smart for him."

Jacob looked down at his feet, kicking up little clouds of dust in the gravel. "It's not so smart hanging around a haunted house," he said. "We could get into big trouble—"

He stopped, interrupted by an angry bellow.

"COME DOWN HERE, YOU THIEVIN' BUNDLE OF HORSE FEATHERS!"

Jacob started to run, and Roddy and Princess followed him. When they raced into Jacob's backyard, they found Uncle Ring glaring up into the oak tree next to the garage and shaking his fist.

"What's wrong?" Jacob gasped. "What's happened?"

"It's that wicked bird!" Uncle Ring roared. "That thievin' Herman! He stole my house key right off the kitchen table and lit out through the window. Lucky I saw where he went!" He pointed into the highest branches of the tree. "You can bet he's there now, laughin' at us!"

They all squinted upward. "I don't see anything," Roddy said.

"Never mind, Uncle Ring," Jacob said soothingly. "Dad probably has an extra key."

"I don't want his extra key," Uncle Ring said crossly. "I want *my* key—the one the wicked bird stole. Get the ladder, Jacob."

"Oh, no!" Now Jacob sounded panicky. "You can't climb the ladder. You'll fall, and Mom will kill me."

Roddy felt, rather than saw, a sudden movement behind him. It was Princess, jumping for the lowest limb of the tree. She missed the first time but caught it the second. From there, she shinnied up the tree quickly.

Uncle Ring's mouth fell open. "Well, now," he began, "you mustn't—"

"What kind of bird is it?" Princess called down. "What color?"

"Yellow and green parakeet," Uncle Ring said, sounding dazed. "Answers to the name of Herman."

Princess scrambled higher in a flurry of thrashing branches. Herman would have to be a pretty stupid bird to stick around through all that commotion, Roddy thought. He moved closer to Jacob, who was watching nervously.

"Why don't you keep Herman in a cage?" Roddy whispered. "You could save everybody a lot of trouble."

Jacob gave him a look. "Can't," he said, his lips barely moving. "He's dead."

Roddy wondered if he'd heard right. "He's *dead*?"

"We had a funeral for him two years ago," Jacob muttered. "He was very old and he died, and my mom and I had a funeral for him. He's buried right there." He pointed at a cluster of pink hollyhocks. "Uncle Ring was at the funeral. He sang 'Amazing Grace.'"

"But if he's dead, and Uncle Ring knows it, why is Princess up there looking for him?" Roddy whispered. "I don't get it."

Jacob rolled his eyes. "Herman keeps coming back," he whispered. "You know—like Mrs. Mortimer. And he steals keys and stuff. Don't tell

Princess," he said hurriedly. "You heard her—she already thinks Uncle Ring is crazy."

"I'm coming down," Princess announced. "There's no key up here. No parakeet either." She dropped lightly to the ground and brushed herself off.

"I'm really sorry I couldn't find your bird," she told Uncle Ring, so sweetly that the boys stared at her. "But I'm sure he's flying around the neighborhood having a good time. Or else," she added cheerfully, "maybe he has a girlfriend and he's taken the key to her. Birds like shiny things."

"Well, that could be," Uncle Ring agreed. His anger seemed to have melted away. "Where did you learn to climb a tree like that, missy?"

"At camp," Princess told him. "I go for a month every summer. It's the best camp in the whole United States. I can climb anything. My dad's going to take me mountain climbing someday. Maybe next week when he comes home."

"Is that so!" Uncle Ring patted her head. "Well, you're one terrific young lady, I can see that. And I'll bet you've roasted lots of wieners at that camp of yours. You can show us how the experts do it."

"Oh, sure," Princess said. "I don't mind. I'll fix one especially for you if you want me to."

She went over to the grill that was set up next to the picnic table, and Uncle Ring followed.

"Why is she being so nice all of a sudden?" Jacob's eyes narrowed with suspicion. "What did you tell her about my uncle?"

"Didn't tell her anything," Roddy said. He started to add, "Cross my heart and hope to die," but thought better of it. "Who knows why she does anything?" he said instead. "Who cares?"

Who cares! That was what he kept saying to himself the rest of the afternoon. When his hot dog fell into the fire and burned, Princess said it was his own fault for using such a thin stick. When Jacob's wiener burst open, she asked him why he had held it so close to the fire. Then, while the boys started over with fresh wieners, she fixed absolutely perfect hot dogs for herself and for Uncle Ring. Between bites she listed the badges she'd earned at camp for outdoor cooking, swimming, horseback riding, and bed making.

Bed making! Roddy rolled his eyes at Jacob. A badge for bed making. Big deal!

"A couple of days ago I saw you walkin' down the street a ways, and I told these two fellas here they better look after you," Uncle Ring said as Princess handed him another perfect hot dog. "But you don't need any lookin' after, do you?"

"No, I don't," Princess said seriously. "I always know what I'm doing."

Ughhhh! Roddy's hot dog churned in his stomach. He followed Jacob into the house to get the ice-cream bars from the freezer.

"What if she wants to sneak around that house again tonight?" Roddy asked. "Are you coming along?"

Jacob took three ice-cream bars out of the freezer and lined them up on a plate. Then he took out one more, tore off the wrapper, and licked the smooth chocolate coating.

"I'm probably going to be busy," he said unhappily.

"Doing what?" Roddy started getting mad all over again. He didn't think he could stand another night alone with Princess under the lilacs.

Jacob picked up the plate and headed back outside without answering.

"At camp a counselor always tells a ghost story after we eat," Princess was saying. "Some of the *little* kids get so scared they won't walk back to their cabins alone, poor things. Can you believe that?"

Uncle Ring helped himself to an ice-cream bar. "Well, now you're talkin' my language," he said comfortably. "You have to remember there's good ghosts and bad ones, missy. I've seen 'em all. You take that house across the street—the one you were lookin' at so hard yesterday afternoon—"

"She doesn't believe in ghosts, Uncle Ring,"

Jacob interrupted. "She doesn't want to hear about that house."

"Yes, I do," Princess said. "What about it?"

"It's haunted, that's what," Uncle Ring said. "A man got himself killed there forty years ago—a gangster most likely. Kept to himself, never spoke to the neighbors, not once! They say he had a fortune, and one night another gangster came lookin' for it. There was a big fight—we all heard 'em yellin'—and the next morning the man who lived there was dead. Stabbed through the heart right in his own living room! His ghost is still there guardin' that fortune."

Roddy swallowed hard. The light he'd seen flickering had been in the living-room window. He waited for Princess to say the whole thing was silly.

"Maybe the other man took it away with him," she said finally. "Anyway, that's a pretty good ghost story," she added, and smiled at Uncle Ring. "Thanks for telling it."

At least she wasn't making fun of him, Roddy thought. But you could tell she hadn't believed a word of it. Why was she being so polite? He found out why later, after they'd said good night to Uncle Ring and Jacob and were walking down the hill.

"That nice old man and his silly ghosts," Princess said. "You and Jacob actually believe him, don't you? I didn't want him to feel bad, so I just kept still. About everything."

Roddy looked at her. "What *everything*?"

"His so-called haunted house. And his bird. It's going to break his heart if he finds out what happened to Herman."

"Now wait a minute," Roddy said. "Herman isn't a real—"

But Princess wouldn't wait. "A hawk got Herman when he flew up in that tree," she said. "Or maybe it was an owl. Anyway, he's dead for sure. I just didn't want to say so."

"How do you know that?" Roddy could hardly get the words out.

Princess reached into the pocket of her shorts and held out her hand. "I know because this is all there is left of him," she said.

Three feathers were scrunched in her palm—two yellow, one green.

8. Night Four

There's something kind of magical about a summer night.

Roddy remembered his mom's words as he and Princess ambled back down the hill. He knew what she meant. After a few hours with Uncle Ring, a person could believe almost anything. A normal person, that is, one who didn't think most other people were silly.

"Those feathers are from some other bird," he said finally. "Herman died two years ago. Jacob told me. Uncle Ring sees Herman's ghost sometimes."

Princess groaned. "You and Jacob are such babies," she said scornfully. "You're lucky I let you come along when I'm detecting."

Oh, sure, lucky, Roddy thought. He wished he'd had a chance to ask Uncle Ring whether he'd seen the tall man in uniform again, but he couldn't ask in front of Princess. He didn't want to hear her say *that* was silly. It was too important.

"Look, your mom's out on the porch again," Princess said a moment later. "I hope she isn't going to sit there for hours and hours."

"She can if she wants," Roddy said coldly. "If it makes her feel good."

"But she doesn't look as if she feels good," Princess said. "I think she should go to bed and sleep."

They were close to home now, and Roddy saw that what Princess said was true. His mom was watching them with a very strange expression.

"We had fun," Princess told her as soon as they reached the porch. "I climbed a tree to look for Jacob's uncle's parakeet, but it wasn't there." She paused. "It was a really tall tree I climbed. Jacob's uncle Ring could hardly believe how brave I was."

Roddy's mom didn't seem to hear. "I had an unexpected visitor this evening," she said. "He just left."

Roddy's heart dropped to his toes. At least, that was how it felt. He knew the army sent someone to tell a soldier's family if he had been killed.

"Wh-who?" He could hardly get the word out.

"It was a policeman," his mom said very quickly, as if she had guessed his thought and was sorry. "He wanted to know if my little girl had

found her cat. He said she and her friend were out looking for the cat in the rain night before last. They told him they lived here."

"Maybe he had the wrong street," Princess suggested. She shoved her fists in the pockets of her shorts and frowned. "Is there anyone around here who has a cat?"

"Not that I know of," Roddy's mom replied. "This policeman said the little girl had a long yellow braid. Any other ideas?" Something in her voice told Roddy she didn't need an answer. And she wasn't just angry. She sounded really tired and even a little bit scared.

"I told him I'd watch out for those kids," she said. "You know, their mothers and fathers probably thought they could trust them to stay in bed and not go wandering around in a storm. They'd be worried sick if they knew the truth."

That was all. Roddy wished she would yell at them, but she didn't. She sounded too tired even to yell. After a while she went inside and turned on the television to get the latest war news. Machine-gun fire and the shriek of an air-raid siren made Roddy shiver.

"Don't bother to knock on the window tonight," he said grimly. "I don't care what you say, I'm not going out."

Somewhere behind him Princess sighed heavily. "Of course not, silly," she said. "Neither am I."

9. Day Five

"This is the worst math test I've ever seen," Miss Miller said. She held up the paper so that the whole class could see the big red F at the top. "I'm ashamed of you, Roddy."

Roddy woke, sweating, from the bad dream. His stomach churned. He lay still, waiting for the sick feeling to go away, but it stayed. Something was wrong. For a moment he couldn't think what it was, and then he remembered. Twice during the night his mom had opened the door at the top of the stairs and pointed a flashlight at his cot to make sure he was still there.

She didn't trust him anymore.

It was all that girl's fault, he thought—that Princess! He thought about what his dad had said before he shipped out—"These are tough times, Roddy. You have to take care of your mom till I get back." He'd been doing fine until Princess came. Now he'd become something his mom had to worry about.

Thunder rumbled in the distance as he pulled on his jeans. Upstairs Roddy found his mom in the kitchen talking on the phone and Princess in the living room playing his new video game. Winning, of course. He glared at her, but she didn't seem to notice.

"Your grandma's sick," she whispered. "She wants your mother to come to Milwaukee and take her to the doctor. We might have to go along."

"That's right," his mom said crisply from the doorway. "I'm certainly not going to leave you here alone all afternoon." Because she doesn't trust us, Roddy thought. She doesn't trust *me*. But he knew that wasn't the only reason. She wouldn't have let them stay home alone, even if that policeman hadn't come back.

"I just talked to Jacob's mother, and she said you can spend the day there if you want. She's going to a church meeting, but she'll be home later. Otherwise you'll have to come along to the doctor's office and wait."

"We'll stay with Jacob," Princess said before Roddy could answer. "His uncle Ring is fun."

"What do you say, Roddy?" his mom asked. "Can I depend on you to do whatever Mrs. Glaubitz tells you?"

Roddy nodded. "Sure. Is Grandma very sick?"

His mom's face softened into a smile. "I don't

think so. But she's frightened, and she's going to worry till her doctor tells her she's okay." She reached out and smoothed Roddy's uncombed hair. "Go eat your breakfast now," she said. "I have to leave in about an hour. I want to get to Grandma's house before the storm breaks."

Maybe today he'd have a chance to ask Uncle Ring about the tall man, Roddy thought. And maybe not. If Princess had decided Uncle Ring was fun, she'd probably stick to him like glue.

Jacob was waiting at the curb when Roddy's mom dropped them off and drove away. Up on the porch, Uncle Ring stared out at the quiet street. He looked as dark and thundery as the sky overhead.

"What's the matter with him?" Princess whispered. "Did he find out his bird is dead?"

Jacob ignored her. "He's been like that all morning," he told Roddy. "He figured out it was forty years ago today that the guy was murdered in that house. Same dark, spooky weather and everything. And some strange guy has been walking up and down the hill all morning."

"I don't see anyone," Princess said. "Is this a joke?"

"No, it's not a joke," Jacob snapped. "Uncle Ring sees him clear as anything, even if we can't. Look!"

They all turned to Uncle Ring. The big man was

leaning forward on the porch swing, his hands on his knees. His head moved slowly from left to right, exactly as if he were watching someone pass by.

"Ha!" he exclaimed, and heaved himself to his feet so suddenly that they all jumped back a step. "I knew it! That's the very one who did the deed. He's going into that house, bold as you please. Returnin' to the scene of the crime after forty years!"

"This is really weird," Princess murmured, and for once Roddy agreed with her. He had thought he wanted to be able to see what Uncle Ring could see, but this was different.

Uncle Ring dropped back into the swing and wiped his forehead with a red bandanna. "I don't like it," he said. "Don't like it at all."

"Uncle Ring—" Jacob began.

His uncle blinked and looked down at them in surprise. "Now where did you come from?" he demanded. "You fellas get up here on the porch with me right now. Mustn't wander around on a day like this."

Jacob tugged Roddy's arm.

"My folks bought two secondhand video games at the church fair," he said. "Want to try them?"

"Cool," Roddy said, and then hesitated. Watching Princess win every game would be bad enough. Listening to her brag about it would be even worse.

"I'd much rather stay here with Uncle Ring,"

Princess said. "I'll help him watch the haunted house."

Jacob scowled, but Uncle Ring seemed pleased. "Glad to have you, missy," he said. "Two sets of eyes are better than one. If there's trouble, we'll sound the alarm."

"She's a real pain," Jacob griped as the boys climbed the stairs to his bedroom. "If she makes fun of Uncle Ring, I'll punch her!"

"If you can catch her," Roddy said, "which I doubt. What kind of trouble is he looking for, anyway?"

Jacob shrugged. "Who knows? My mom says Uncle Ring's life is full of adventures. He sees more than anybody, just sitting on the porch."

Princess liked lots of adventures, too, Roddy thought, even though she and Uncle Ring were so different. She was always looking for a big adventure, and right now she was ruining his life to get it.

"She'll be gone in two more days, right?" Jacob asked suddenly, as if he had read Roddy's mind.

"Right," Roddy said, and relaxed a little. "Just today and part of tomorrow. Her stepmother is coming for her tomorrow afternoon."

"I'll be glad when she goes home," Jacob said soberly. "She makes me feel like a big nothing."

The first video game was boring. Roddy could see why its owner had given it away. The other one was pretty good. They were just starting to play it a second time when Uncle Ring's bellow from down-stairs stopped them.

"JACOB! You fellas come down here and eat. Your mama left a whole plateful of sandwiches in case she didn't get home before lunch. You come now. Herman's around again, just looking for some-thing to steal."

"Princess says Herman is dead," Roddy whis-pered as they trudged downstairs. "She found some feathers when she climbed that tree."

"Feathers maybe, but not Herman's feathers," Jacob whispered back. "I *told* you he was dead myself. He just doesn't stay dead for Uncle Ring. She better not argue with him."

"She won't. She—" Roddy stopped for a second to listen. The house was too quiet. Then he hurtled the last three steps in one leap and dashed into the kitchen. Uncle Ring sat at the table munching a sandwich and swatting the air above his head.

"Dratted bird," he growled. "Almost got my pickle that time!"

"Where—where is she?" Roddy could hardly get the words out. "Where's Princess?"

Uncle Ring stopped chewing. "What d'ya mean, boy? She went upstairs to play those fool games with you. Said she's better at those games than anyone."

"No," Roddy said. "She isn't upstairs." He

looked at Jacob, who was watching his great-uncle uneasily.

The old man pushed back his chair and pounded the table with a burly fist. "Then where is she?" he roared. "She shouldn't be running around by herself today." His face was bright red. He looked as if he might explode on the spot.

"Don't get excited, Uncle Ring," Jacob begged. "You're not supposed to get excited."

"Maybe she's in the bathroom," Roddy suggested. "Hey, Princess!"

The house was quiet, except for the soft *tap-tap* of raindrops on the windows. "I know!" Jacob sounded desperate. "I bet she went down the alley to get something from your house."

Uncle Ring leaned back in his chair. "Get what?" he demanded. "A doll, maybe?"

The thought of Princess playing with a doll would have made Roddy laugh out loud if he hadn't been so worried. He *knew* where she was. Somehow, she had crossed Hilltop Drive to the haunted house without Uncle Ring seeing her. It just proved what she had told Roddy two days before at breakfast. She never gave up.

Jacob must have guessed where she was, too. "You'd better go and help her find the doll," he told Roddy. "I'll stay with Uncle Ring."

Uncle Ring's face had faded to its usual color, but he still looked upset. "Use the alley, boy," he ordered. "Nobody should be out on the street today. Not today!" He shook his head grimly.

Roddy ran. The screen door slammed behind him as he raced across the backyard. When he reached the alley, he hesitated, but only for a moment. How would Princess cross Hilltop? If she crossed at the bottom of the street, Uncle Ring might see her. She'd have to go up the alley and cross at the top, where Hilltop made a sharp dip. All she'd have to do then was cut between a couple of houses and go down the alley to the haunted house.

As he ran, Roddy thought of what he would say to Princess when he caught up with her.

"You're a liar and a sneak!"

"You almost made Uncle Ring sick!"

"You make me sick!"

The words were right there, waiting to be said, when he reached the garage of the haunted house. It was covered with the same shabby brown shingles as the house. When he peered through a dusty window, he saw that Princess had been right. No one could park a car in that junk-filled place.

The backyard was littered with junk, too. Roddy crouched and looked hard at the long row of bushes that ran all the way to the street. She would be under there, he thought, waiting and watching.

That was her emmo. But what did she expect to see now? The car without headlights only came after dark. There was no one in the house now except— he shuddered—no one except the ghost of a man who'd been murdered and the ghost of the man who killed him.

Roddy flattened himself against the side of the garage as the light sprinkle turned into a hard rain. It was probably a lot drier under the bushes, he thought furiously. If Princess could see him, she'd be snickering.

He took a step forward and crouched, ready to dash to the row of bushes himself. First, though, he had to be sure no one—no *thing*—was watching from the windows in the back of the house. . . .

"Hey!" Roddy almost yelled out loud at what he saw. Not a shadowy figure staring at him through streaming glass, but something much worse. Across a yard cluttered with boxes and broken-down furniture, there was a rickety table with a wooden crate on top of it. The table was below a window, and the window was open just wide enough for a skinny kid to squeeze through. Roddy knew what that meant, as surely as if he had seen it happen.

Princess had gone inside.

10. Day Five

(continued)

Roddy had never felt like this before. First-day-in-a-new-school was one kind of aloneness. Watching your dad swing his duffel bag into the backseat of a car and be driven away was another, much worse, kind. This aloneness was different. This time he had to decide right then, all by himself, what to do.

He could run away. Pretend he didn't know where Princess was. Wait to see what happened.

Or he could go for help. Not at Jacob's house, though. Uncle Ring might actually explode or something if he knew Princess was inside the haunted house. He'd have to go home, call the police from there, tell them—NO! Another bad idea! Princess would be arrested for breaking into a house. He pictured her in handcuffs, wearing one of those baggy orange jail outfits. Then he pictured his mom crying and saying it was all her fault for leaving that sweet little girl alone.

Or—Roddy groaned at this third idea—he could get her out of the house himself. His stomach told him this was the worst idea of all, but what else could he do? Before his mom and Jacob's mom and Uncle Ring found out what a dumb thing she had done, he had to find her and tell her himself.

He ran across the yard and scrambled onto the rickety table. His squishy-wet sneakers slipped when he tried to step up onto the crate. Even his shoes didn't want to go in there! He kicked them off. Then he grabbed the window ledge, pulled himself up, and peered inside.

The room was almost empty. It was a shabby old kitchen with a table, one chair, and cupboards that stretched up to the ceiling. One cupboard door gaped emptily under the sink. A microwave oven stood on the counter.

Roddy stared into the dimness so hard that his eyes ached. He didn't know what he'd expected to see—a hulking figure, maybe, with arms outstretched and a bloody knife in one hand. But the figure wasn't there, and neither was Princess. If he was going to find her, he had to go inside.

He swung one leg over the sill, then the other. When he stood up, he felt dizzy. The house didn't want him in it, he could feel that. He stood close to the window and looked around.

There was an open door to his left leading

down into an inky black cellar. Straight ahead a little hallway led into the rest of the house. The living room would be down that hallway—the living room where long ago people had found a dead man lying on the floor.

Where was Princess hiding? He took a step, and the floor creaked. It was the loudest creak he had ever heard. He couldn't look away from the hallway. Whoever—whatever—was in the living room must know now that he was in the kitchen. He could feel the waves of meanness Uncle Ring had told them about. They washed over him, making his knees shake and turning his brain to mush. Then he heard footsteps. They weren't skinny-girl footsteps, but heavy ones. They came from overhead. *Step, ssshhh, step, ssshhh*—someone big was pushing something smaller across the floor.

GO! Roddy didn't just think the word, he felt it like an electric shock that sent him scrambling over the window ledge. One foot kicked the crate, knocking it aside. He dangled there for a second, then dropped. The table tilted, and he hit the ground running.

GO! GO! GO! The word pounded in his head until—halfway across the yard—he sloshed through a puddle and nearly fell. Then another word drowned it out. SHOES! His shoes were lying on the ground under the window.

Later Roddy decided that going back for the shoes had been the hardest thing of all. He wanted to keep running, but the small part of his brain that was still working said he had to go back. How could he ever explain losing his shoes?

He dashed back and grabbed the shoes without taking his eyes off the open window. The *thing* that had been walking upstairs had had plenty of time to come down to the kitchen, but the window remained empty. He turned and ran back across the yard to the alley.

Now what? He raced up the hill, crossed the street, and started down his own alley before he felt safe enough to stop and put on his shoes.

"Man, where've you been?"

Roddy straightened up and saw Jacob coming toward him, looking worried.

"I couldn't find her," Roddy said fast before Jacob could ask. "She's in the haunted house and I went in after her, but I couldn't find her!"

Jacob stared. "You went *in* that house," he repeated. "I don't believe it."

"Well, I did," Roddy said. He was suddenly too tired to argue. "Uncle Ring is right. There is another ghost! I heard him. He was upstairs walking around—looking for the money, maybe. Princess might be up there, too. She might even be—be—" He couldn't say the word.

Jacob shook his head. "I can't believe you went in there," he said slowly. "Come on." He turned and pushed open the backyard gate.

Roddy followed him across the yard and around the side of the house because he didn't know what else to do.

"Your turn," said a voice from the front porch. "I guess I'm going to win again."

"Looks like." Uncle Ring yawned noisily. "But I'll beat you next time, missy, you'll see."

Roddy stopped short, and Jacob turned to him with a grin. "She wasn't in the haunted house, man. She wanted to take Uncle Ring's mind off it, so she went back to your place for her Chinese checkers board."

Roddy blinked. "Her Chinese checkers board?" he said weakly. "*My* Chinese checkers board!"

"Well, sure," Jacob agreed. "Whatever. She couldn't find it at first—that's why she was gone awhile. But it was a good idea—they've been playing ever since she got back. Uncle Ring's having such a good time he hasn't even asked why you didn't come back with her." He gave Roddy a poke. "You were the only one in the haunted house, goofy—you and the ghosts. Which makes me right, right? That girl can make you do something crazy when she isn't even trying!"

11. Night Five

"Your mother just called from Milwaukee. She'll be home in about a half hour." Mrs. Glaubitz set a plate of chocolate chip cookies on the table and poured glasses of lemonade. "Jacob, go out on the porch and see whether Princess and Uncle Ring want a snack."

"I do, but Uncle Ring doesn't," said Princess from the doorway. "He fell asleep all of a sudden, while I was getting the checkerboard ready for another game."

Jacob's mom smiled. "Wonderful!" she said, and gave Princess a hug. "He was having a very bad day, and you calmed him down. You're a dear, sweet girl."

"That's okay," Princess said in a dear, sweet voice. "I like to help people. We don't have uncles in our family. Or aunts. Or anybody, except my dad and my stepmother. There's just me."

Roddy wondered if she was going to tell Mrs.

Glaubitz about her poor lost kitty. He thought he might throw up if she did.

Later, as they tiptoed past Uncle Ring and started down the hill toward home, the dear, sweet voice was gone.

"So where were *you?*" Princess demanded. "Jacob whispered that you might have gone to the burglar's house, but he was just being silly. You wouldn't dare."

"I would, too, dare," Roddy said. "I did! I even went inside. There was an open window in the back and a table underneath it, so I thought you were in there. I was going to—"

"Going to what?" Princess interrupted. "Were you going to save me?" She was laughing at him!

"I was going to yell at you," Roddy admitted. "You could get in big trouble breaking into somebody's house."

Princess stopped laughing. "Well, sure you could," she said. "But I was playing Chinese checkers with Uncle Ring, remember? I just hope nobody saw you. You could have spoiled everything."

"Nobody saw me." Roddy was about to tell her about the ghostly footsteps when his mom's car passed them. She blew the horn and waved without slowing down. They watched as she parked in front of the house and ran up the steps to the mailbox.

She glanced through a handful of envelopes and then stuffed them into her jacket pocket.

"No letter from your father," Princess said. "That's too bad."

Roddy glanced at her, surprised. She really sounded sorry. "It's not his fault," he said. "Maybe the letter got lost. Or maybe he's . . ."

"Busy." Princess finished the sentence for him. "I think he's busy. When you're really busy you don't have time to write."

She sounded as if she knew all about people who were too busy to write. Then she grabbed his arm and pulled.

"Hurry up, slowpoke," she snapped. "Move!"

Roddy shook off her hand. For one moment there she had sounded like an almost nice person, but the moment had passed. He took a deep breath. Only one more night and part of a day, and she'd be gone.

After supper they all sat on the porch steps for a while. The rain had stopped, but a warm, wet breeze brushed their faces. Once in a while a streak of lightning flashed across the sky, making Hilltop Drive spooky in the bursts of light.

"When the doctor told Grandma she wasn't really sick, she was ready to celebrate," Roddy's mom told them with a yawn. "The traffic was terrible, but we stopped for frozen custard cones on our way back to her apartment. I wished you both were with us."

"I guess it's a good thing we stayed here," Princess told her. "Jacob's uncle Ring was having a bad day, and I made him feel better."

Roddy's mom leaned back against the porch railing, and Roddy could tell she was half asleep.

"I know it's early, but if I go to bed now," she said, "can I depend on you two to take care of yourselves?"

"Oh, sure," Princess said quickly. "You go to bed right this minute. You look really tired."

Roddy's mom smiled, a sad little smile. "No funny stuff, Roddy?" She looked at him directly and waited for an answer.

"We'll be okay," he said. "Don't worry."

After she'd gone inside, they sat for a couple of minutes, just staring into the dark. A flash of lightning lit the quivering branches of the willow tree across the street.

Princess stood up. "You know what? I'm tired, too," she said with a phony-sounding yawn.

Roddy jumped to his feet and stood in front of the door. "You'd better not try anything tonight," he said. "You'd just better not! You promised my mom."

"I promised I'd take care of myself," Princess

said, ducking under his outstretched arm. "And I will. Don't you worry about me, little boy."

A whole hour passed before Roddy saw her. He'd been sitting on the edge of his basement cot all that time, trying to decide what he would do if she sneaked out again. He had almost begun to believe she really had gone to bed, when her skinny legs flashed by the window.

No funny stuff, his mom had said.

The trouble was, she didn't know the real Princess at all. "That girl thinks she's so smart," he grumbled to himself as he headed up the stairs. "She thinks she knows everything, but she doesn't. She doesn't know that the ghost Uncle Ring saw on the street this morning might still be prowling around the haunted house this afternoon. She doesn't know that!"

The ghost of a killer, he thought with a shudder. What would a killer ghost do if he caught a smart-aleck kid poking around where she didn't belong?

"If you're coming you have to do exactly what I tell you," Princess said. "Every minute! You have to fol-low the plan."

"What plan?" Roddy looked up the hill, but Jacob was nowhere in sight. They had reached the end of the driveway at the side of the haunted house, and Princess started crawling under the lilac bushes before she answered.

"We're going inside to look around. It's my last chance."

Roddy ducked under the bushes and crawled. At once his hands and knees were soaked, and dripping leaves brushed his nose. He could hardly breathe.

"We'll go in through that window you used," Princess went on. "The burglar must have left it open the last time he was here. And then we'll search the whole house."

"We can't!" Roddy protested. He was desperate now. "You heard Uncle Ring this morning—what he said is true! There's a ghost in there. I heard him walking upstairs. He could still be around."

Princess pushed a branch aside and let it flop back in Roddy's face. "No, you didn't, silly. You didn't hear anything. Uncle Ring likes to make up scary stories and you like to believe them. There's no such thing as a ghost."

"If we get caught, we could go to jail," Roddy said, smothering a sneeze. He felt hot and cold at the same time and wondered whether he was dying. If he died, here under the bushes, no one could blame him for letting Princess get into trouble.

"We are *not* going to get caught," Princess said. "We're going to be heroes. Just do what I tell you."

They passed the side door and crawled on to the backyard. Princess poked her head out from under the bushes and pointed her flashlight at the back of the house.

"I see the window," she said. The beam of light dropped. "And there's the table. But it's not nearly high enough. You never climbed through the window standing on that." The flashlight beam dropped lower. "Okay, there's a big box on the ground. It was on the table, right? Help me put it back."

Roddy gritted his teeth. For a moment he'd hoped she wouldn't see the box.

"I'll go in first," Princess said. "I'll let you know when it's safe. *If* you want to come in, that is. Or you can just stay here like a scared rabbit and watch for a glimmer in the window." She snickered.

Until that moment Roddy had thought there might be some way he could avoid going back into the haunted house. Now he knew he would have to go inside with Princess or feel like a scared rabbit forever.

"I'm coming!" he snapped. "Hurry up!"

A minute later they were both standing in the kitchen. Roddy switched on his flashlight and looked around. The tall cupboards loomed eerily in the dark.

"We have to do this as fast as possible," Princess

said in a low voice. "Just in case the burglar comes back early tonight."

Roddy almost dropped his flashlight. He hadn't thought of that.

"I'll go upstairs and look around," she went on, sounding as if she broke into houses every night. "You check the first floor. Search the closets and the cupboards—anywhere a burglar could hide his loot."

What kind of loot? Roddy wondered, but Princess was already tiptoeing down the hall. Her yellow braid gleamed in the beam of his flashlight as she turned and started up the stairs. He was alone.

Closets and cupboards—he looked around at the tall cupboards and knew he couldn't open even one of them without making a noise. And if he made a noise, something might hear him—some dead thing that had been waiting and watching in the living room for forty years.

He switched off his light and started down the hall, holding his breath every time the floor creaked. He passed the stairs just opposite the side door. Then the wall ended, and he knew he was in the living room. His hands were clammy as he searched for the switch of his flashlight.

Suddenly, a flash of lightning filled the room with cold white light. It lasted only a second, but that was long enough. The thing he had feared—the ghost of the murdered man—sat upright in a battered armchair. Its legs were stretched out, and its arms hung limply over the arms of the chair. Its mouth sagged open, and the eyes—horrible eyes, like black holes—stared straight ahead.

"Who's there?" a voice snarled in the dark.

Roddy yelped in terror. Then he whirled around and raced back to the kitchen.

12. Night Five

(continued)

Afterward, Roddy couldn't remember diving into the space under the sink and pulling the door shut behind him. One moment he'd been racing toward the open window with heavy footsteps getting closer behind him. The next, he had wrapped himself around the U-shaped drainpipe and was trying hard not to breathe.

"Come on!" the voice growled. "No use hiding— I know you're here!"

Of course he knew, Roddy thought. How could you fool a ghost?

The footsteps shuffled around the kitchen. A cupboard door was flung open, then another. Roddy screwed his eyes shut and waited.

Another sound began and stopped, outside the house but close by. A car door opened and closed. Roddy almost groaned out loud. That had to be the

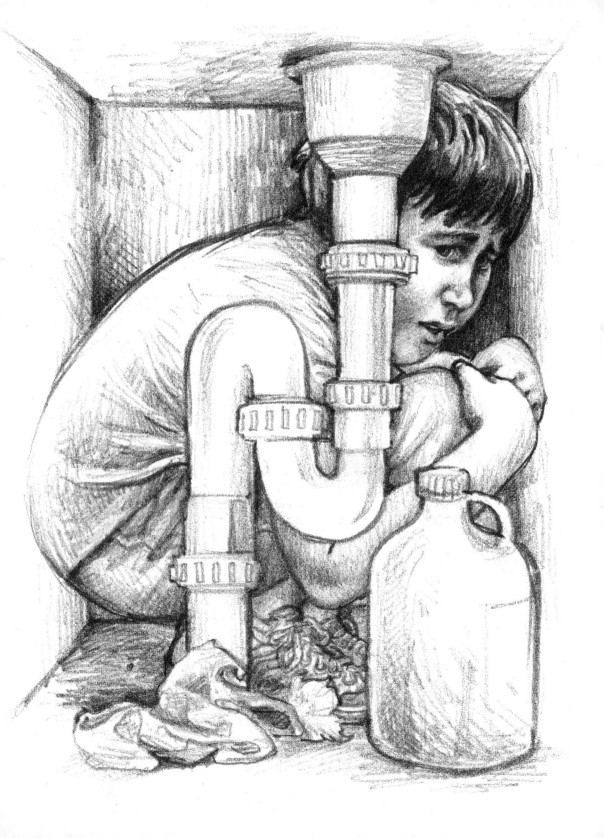

burglar arriving early. He could almost hear Princess saying "I told you so."

The footsteps moved back to the hallway, and voices mumbled and sputtered. Roddy could make out only a word here and there. ". . . someone in here . . . sleeping . . . not my fault . . . check upstairs . . . I'll take the basement. . . ."

Roddy's mind was in a muddle. The ghost and the burglar were actually talking to each other, and now the ghost sounded like a real person. One of them, he couldn't be sure which, was starting down the basement steps, while the other one went upstairs.

The kitchen was empty. He waited a second or two to be sure. Then he opened the cupboard door a crack. The open window was just a few feet away. If he moved fast and was very quiet, he could get away.

He was so scared he had one leg over the windowsill, toes reaching for the box, when he remembered Princess trapped upstairs. She'd said she could take care of herself, but that was just talk—dumb talk. Princess talk. Right now she had to be as frightened as he was.

He scrambled back inside and ran to the foot of the stairs. A hulking figure carrying a flashlight had nearly reached the top. Roddy yelled "Hey!" but the word was just a squeak. "Hey!" He tried it again, much louder. "I'm down here!"

And then everything happened at once. The man on the stairs turned with a startled grunt. His flashlight shot into the air, and a second later he hurtled headfirst down the stairs. Roddy jumped to one side, and at the same moment the outside door behind him burst open. The falling man landed with a bone-jarring thump and lay still.

Someone tall stepped into the hall and pointed a flashlight at the man on the floor. Then the light shot upward to Roddy's face.

"Good grief, it's you again!" said a familiar voice. "Don't tell me, let me guess. It's another stormy night and you've lost your poor little kitty."

13. Night Five

(still continued)

The man on the floor moved and groaned. Roddy jumped back.

"Okay, young fellow," the policeman said. "Speak up! What's going on here?"

"Well..." Before Roddy could think of an answer, a clear voice from the top of the stairs answered for him.

"It's all right, officer," Princess said. "That man on the floor is a dangerous burglar. I pushed him down the stairs."

The flashlight beam shot upward as Princess started down. "I had to do it," she announced. "They would have killed us if they caught us."

"They?" the policeman repeated. "Who else—?"

"There's another one in the b-b-basement," Roddy stammered. "Looking for us."

A second policeman stepped through the door and switched on an overhead light.

"Down there." Roddy pointed. The second policeman headed across the kitchen toward the basement, switching on lights as he went. He returned almost at once, pushing a slouching, sour-faced man ahead of him.

The captive's eyes widened when he saw Roddy and Princess. "Kids!" he exclaimed. "A couple of fool kids! I should have known. Nobody's house is safe these days."

"Are you saying this is your house?" the first policeman demanded. He glanced at the almost empty kitchen. "Sure doesn't look as if anyone lives here."

"They don't!" Princess exclaimed. "Not really. They just hide their loot here. That's what we were looking for, see? We were helping the police. Only we thought there was only one burglar, not two."

The man on the floor sat up, rubbing his head. "I rent this place," he growled. "You can call the owner if you don't believe me. These kids broke in and I want them arrested."

Roddy felt seriously sick. If the two men really lived here, then he and Princess were in trouble. Big trouble! They would almost certainly go to jail. His mom would never forgive him for sneaking out again when she had trusted him, and his dad—NO! He couldn't even bear to think about what his dad would say.

The first policeman shook his head. "What we're going to do is this," he said. "We're all taking a ride down to the station to sort this out." He helped the fallen man to his feet. "Let's go."

"Hey, not us!" the man protested. "Why should we go? This is our house. These kids are trouble-makers. I told you, I want them arrested."

"We're all going," the policeman said firmly. "Take 'em," he told his partner.

The man stumbled out the door, and Roddy started to follow. He wished he'd never been born. Even Princess must see what a mess they were in now. He looked back, and there she was, still standing on the bottom step of the staircase.

She was *smiling*.

He knew then that Jacob had been right all along. Princess really was crazy. He should have made his mom understand that. He should have told *somebody*. Now it was too late.

"Before we go you should see something, officer," Princess said. Roddy shivered. The dear, sweet voice was back. "It's very important." She turned and started upstairs.

"Now what?" the policeman asked suspiciously. "You've found your cat?"

When Princess didn't answer he shrugged, grabbed Roddy by the shoulder, and climbed the stairs after her.

There were several open doors off the small landing at the top. Princess stepped through one of them. With her flashlight she found a wall switch and turned it on.

"All right, you can come in now," she said grandly. Roddy cringed. She sounded like the hostess at a surprise party, he thought. Crazy, crazy, crazy!

He followed the policeman into the room. The floor was bare, and there was nothing to see except boxes. They were stacked from the floor to the ceiling against each wall. Every box was stamped PROPERTY OF THE UNITED STATES ARMY.

The policeman pushed back his hat and said, "Well, I'll be a cockapoo's cousin!"

"Yeah," Roddy breathed. "Me too."

Princess swung around on tiptoe. "And there's more in the other bedroom," she said. "I checked." Her face glowed pink and her eyes sparkled. Roddy thought she didn't look like the same person who had been ruining his life for a week. She looked happy.

Jacob, his mom and dad, and Uncle Ring were waiting out on the sidewalk in front of the house. They all looked relieved when they saw Roddy and Princess coming toward them. Roddy searched for his mom among the few neighbors gathered nearby, but he couldn't find her.

"Praise be!" Uncle Ring shouted. "You're all

right! Whatever possessed you to go into that terrible place? I warned you—didn't I warn you?"

"Yeah," Roddy mumbled. "We're sorry, Uncle Ring. It just happened—"

"No, it did *not* just happen," Princess interrupted. "We had to do it to look for the loot, Uncle Ring. The treasure! And guess what—"

"Never mind!" the policeman interrupted. He paused while the squad car pulled out of the driveway with the two burglars in the backseat. "Are these kids yours?" he asked the Glaubitzes. "I need to talk to them now—someplace quiet."

Mr. Glaubitz looked dazed, but Jacob's mom answered quickly. "They're our son's friends," she said. "You can talk to them at our house. Roddy's mother must be fast asleep or she'd be here by now, poor woman." She frowned at Roddy. "I hate to wake her with all she has to worry about, but I'll call. My husband will fetch her."

The little group started up the street toward Jacob's house in silence. Even Princess was quiet at first. Then she said, "Roddy's mom will be proud of us, don't you think?"

No one answered.

"Well, my dad will be proud," she went on loudly. "Proud as anything! Just wait till I tell him!"

For Roddy, the next hours were a painful blur. Over and over again, the policeman made them explain why they had been "playing detective" in the haunted house. How many times had they gone inside? When? What had they seen and heard while they were in there?

Princess did most of the talking, but Roddy had to tell how and why he'd entered the house by himself that afternoon. All the time the questions went on, his mom stared at him, white-faced, as if she couldn't believe what she was hearing. She sat on the couch between Mrs. Glaubitz and Uncle Ring. Mrs. Glaubitz kept patting her hand. Uncle Ring fell asleep.

The doorbell made them all jump. Mr. Glaubitz went to see who was there. He came back with three strangers.

"Reporters from the *Sentinel,*" he announced. "They want to take pictures."

"Oh, good!" Princess jumped up. "I can tell them everything that happened, if you want me to."

"Come back later," the policeman barked, motioning the reporters toward the door. "We're busy now."

When at last he said they could all go home, Roddy could hardly believe it. He and Princess followed his mom and Mr. Glaubitz outside, and Jacob came, too.

"Why did you call the police?" Roddy whispered. "How did you know we were in the haunted house?"

"I didn't call them," Jacob whispered back. "Uncle Ring did. I heard him go downstairs, so I went after him to see what was up. He was calling nine-one-one."

"But why?" Roddy repeated. "Why did he call?"

"It was Mrs. Mortimer," Jacob explained. "He said someone was throwing pebbles at his window, and when he looked down, there she was. He said she was jumping up and down, she was so upset, and she kept pointing at the haunted house. He knew something bad must be happening. So he called."

That was weird, Roddy decided, but no more weird than everything else that had happened that night.

"I thought I saw the dead man in the living room," he said. Even now the memory made him feel cold. "Only he wasn't dead. The policeman thinks he and the other one were taking turns staying there. To guard the—the loot."

Jacob shook his head. "You know what, man? You could have been shot. Or stabbed. Or something. . . . Is that girl really going home tomorrow? Are you sure?"

Roddy yawned. "Her stepmom's coming for her."

"Well, if she doesn't go, call me," Jacob said, "so I can stay in the house all day. I never want to see her again. Not ever! Next time Mrs. Mortimer might not be around when we need her."

14. Day Six

"I want to talk to you, Jane," Roddy's mom said, when Princess finally came into the kitchen the next morning. "Roddy and I have already discussed what happened. He knows how I feel. I'd like you to know, too."

"I'm really sorry if we worried you," Princess said quickly. She slid into a chair and reached for a piece of toast. "Why did you call me Jane?"

"Because this is a serious talk, and that's your real name. It's a perfectly nice name, you know. Someday you may write a book or climb a mountain or discover a cure for a terrible disease, and then everyone will know Jane Thornberry."

Roddy looked at her in surprise. Did she really think Princess might do stuff like that?

"I thought you were going to yell at me," Princess said. "Did you yell at Roddy? It wasn't his fault as much as mine. It was my idea to catch the burglars."

"I didn't yell," Roddy's mom said. "And I have a pretty good idea of how this all happened. What I want to say is, you're never going to do any of those special things when you grow up, Jane, if you don't start using your brain now."

Princess's face turned red. "I do use my brain," she protested. "All the time."

"You sneaked out of a home where you were a trusted guest," Roddy's mom said. "You broke into someone else's house. You put yourself in the worst kind of danger from those awful men."

"But they were stealing *tons* of stuff from the Army of the United States of America," Princess argued. "Aren't you glad we caught them? I bet your husband—"

"That's all I wanted to say," Roddy's mom said. "Now, you'd better eat your breakfast. I have a feeling this is going to be a full day."

The doorbell rang, and Roddy ran to answer it, glad of the chance to get away. The reporters from the *Sentinel* waited on the porch. Behind them were other people with notebooks and cameras.

"Hi, kid, we're back," a freckled man said with a grin. "We're here to interview a couple of young heroes."

Roddy heard his mother sigh behind him. "We were expecting you," she said. "You might as well come in and get it over with."

95

She led the way into the living room, and they all trooped after her. Princess was already there, sitting in the big armchair, her hands folded on her knees. Roddy noticed for the first time that she was dressed up—crisp yellow shorts, a yellow and white top. Her shiny hair matched the shorts. Oh, yeah, he thought. Dear. Sweet.

A camera flashed, then another one. "Okay, Sunbeam," said the man with the freckles. "Why don't you tell us all about it?"

"You should have heard her," Roddy told Jacob later. "Boy, did she tell them!" They were sitting on the Glaubitzes' front porch licking frozen Milky Way bars.

"I'll bet," Jacob said. "Did she tell them you only went along to try to keep her out of trouble?"

"She said I was a good helper."

"Huh!" Jacob made a face.

"She said another little boy helped her, too," Roddy added slyly. "Your name is going to be in the paper."

"Little boy!" Jacob groaned. "My folks don't even know I had anything to do with this. Uncle Ring's going to chew my ear off when he finds out." He took a big bite of his Milky Way. "Has she gone yet? I hope."

"Not yet," Roddy replied. "My mom helped

pack her stuff, and now they're making more chocolate chip cookies. Princess wants fresh ones for her dad."

They sat quietly for a while. Roddy felt trickles of sweat run down between his shoulders. This week had been like one long storm, he thought. Now it was over.

"Hey, take a look at that!" Jacob pointed at a sleek blue convertible that had come over the top of the hill. A pretty woman with long blonde hair was driving. They watched the car roll down the street and glide to a stop in front of Roddy's house.

"Gotta go," Roddy said. "I'm supposed to be there to say good-bye. See you later."

"Right," Jacob said. "Wouldn't you know she'd go home in a convertible?"

When Roddy went into his house, Princess was already describing their adventures to her stepmother. She was doing the tiptoe thing again—whirling around as she talked.

"My picture's going to be in the paper, and I'll be on TV news tonight! Isn't that great?"

Linda rolled her eyes. "Well, you certainly were a fun guest, weren't you?" she said with a sideways grin at Roddy's mom. "Your father is going to be shocked."

Princess stopped in the middle of a twirl. "Oh, no!" she exclaimed. "He's going to be *happy*—he likes it when I do things. When will he be home—tomorrow?"

Linda's grin faded. "You can call him tomorrow if you want to," she said. "He's still in Switzerland."

"But I want to tell him here," Princess whined. "Not on the phone. *Here!*"

"Well, you can't," Linda told her. "Not for a while. Something has come up." She took a deep breath. "He'll be home for Thanksgiving, for sure. After you go back to boarding school, I'm going to fly to Switzerland to meet him for some skiing. I can take the newspaper story with me, if you want me to. And maybe we can tape the television news for him tonight."

Princess sat down hard. Her eyes glittered, and Roddy wondered if she was going to cry. Couldn't be, he decided. Princess would never cry.

"All right, we'd better get going," Linda continued briskly. She thanked Roddy's mom for her help, and then they all walked out to the car. Roddy said good-bye, and Princess wiggled her fingers at him. She hugged his mom before she slumped into the passenger seat.

"I'm very glad we had a chance to meet, Princess," Roddy's mom said. "I mean that. You are a remarkable person."

"I know," Princess said in a small voice. "Thanks for letting me stay here."

And then they were gone.

When the car turned the corner at the foot of the hill, Roddy's mom threw her arm around his shoulders and pulled him close. "Do you know how very sad that was, Roddy?" she asked. "Do you understand?"

"I guess," Roddy said. But he wasn't sure.

"I can see now that this whole dangerous business was supposed to be a huge surprise for her father," she said. "To impress him—like the chocolate chip cookies, only much bigger."

Roddy looked up the hill. Jacob was giving a thumbs-up as the convertible disappeared.

"It's not so sad," he argued. "She can still surprise her dad, can't she? Just not right away."

His mom nodded. "Not right away," she repeated. "I don't think he's in any great hurry to come home, do you? That's the sad part."

15. Day Six

(continued)

After lunch Roddy went to his room to put things back in the dresser drawer where they belonged—his flashlight and his two best video games, the jeans with the holes in the knees that he liked better than the new pair, and the Good Citizen medal he'd won the last day at his old school. When he finished, the room looked the way it was supposed to again, only neater.

He was poking around in the closet to make sure Princess hadn't left any girl stuff behind, when he heard the doorbell ring. Then, after a moment, he heard his mom say "Oh!" That was all, just a funny little "Oh!" For some reason Roddy didn't understand, it sent a shiver down his spine.

He ran to the top of the stairs. The front door was open and his mom was standing there with her back to him, staring down at something he couldn't see. When she turned around, he saw that she was crying and laughing at the same time.

"Not one letter, Roddy," she said in a shaky voice. "Three of them! The mail carrier was so excited he made a special trip to bring them first. Come on down—we'll read them together!"

Roddy threw one leg over the banister and slid to the bottom. His mom had told him not to do that because he might fall off or get slivers you-know-where, but this time she was too excited to notice. She was already sitting on the couch ripping open one of the envelopes.

She had left the front door open. As Roddy leaned out to pull the screen shut, he saw someone passing Jacob's house. It was a tall man, walking fast. He might have been wearing a uniform—it was hard to tell in the glare of the sun. Roddy watched until he disappeared over the top of the hill.

"Come on, Roddy!" His mom was laughing out loud. "You have to hear this!"

Roddy closed the door. He wondered if he'd just seen Uncle Ring's tall fella in a uniform. It could be, or maybe it was the mail carrier hurrying to make up for lost time. He guessed he'd never know, but either way, they had the letters.

16. Day Seven

The first letter was Roddy's favorite. His mom let him take part of it to read to Jacob, as long as he promised to bring it right back.

He found Jacob in the backyard weeding peas and onions. Uncle Ring was asleep on the picnic table.

"Hey, we got letters," Roddy said, trying to sound calm. "Three of 'em."

Jacob handed Roddy a fat pea pod and picked one for himself. "I know." He grinned. "My mom's been smiling and singing hymns ever since your mother called."

"I brought one along in case you'd like to hear it," Roddy said.

Jacob looked surprised. "Okay," he said. He wiped his sweaty face with his sleeve and rocked back on his heels to listen.

"'Sorry about the long time between letters,'" Roddy read. "'I've been on special assignment and there was no way to get in touch. But I thought

about you all the time and tried real hard to imagine what you might be doing.'"

"There now! Didn't I tell you?" Uncle Ring said, not asleep after all. "Just like I said."

Roddy turned the page. "Listen to this," he said. "This is the best part." He read louder, so that Uncle Ring would hear every word:

"'We found a dog, a scrawny little puppy, and we brought her back with us to the place where we're staying. I never realized before how much a dog can help when you're feeling down, which I was. If I can't bring Princess with me when I come home, I'll find somebody here to take good care of her. Whatever happens, we're going to have a dog of our own some day. That's a promise.'"

Uncle Ring chuckled.

Jacob fell back on the grass. "Princess!" he exclaimed. "Does it really say that he calls his dog Princess?"

Roddy nodded. "That's what it says."

"Maybe you could change her name to something else," Jacob said. "I bet your dad wouldn't care."

Roddy had thought about that in bed the night before and had made up his mind.

"Princess is okay with me," he said. "But we might as well take that old doghouse back where we found it, right? If we have a dog called Princess, you know she's going to want to sleep in my bed."